B

# Pat Zietlow Miller

## Illustrated by Jen Hill

To two of the kindest people I know — my sister,
Pam Wells, and my friend Ellen Lawrence — P. Z. M.

To my Mum and dad — J. H.

First published in the USA 2018 by Roaring Book Press
First published in the UK 2020 by Macmillan Children's Books
an imprint of Pan Macmillan
The Smithson, 6 Briset Street, London EC1M 5NR
Associated companies throughout the world
www.panmacmillan.com

ISBN (PB): 978-1-5290-4190-3

Text copyright © Pat Zietlow Miller 2018
Illustrations copyright © Jen Hill 2018

The rights of Pat Zietlow Miller and Jen Hill to be identified as the author and illustrator of this work
have been asserted in accordance with the Copyright, Designs and Patents Act of 1988.

1 3 5 7 9 8 6 4 2

A CIP catalogue record for this book is available from the British Library.

Printed in China

Tanisha spilled grape juice yesterday.

All
over
her
new
dress.

Everyone laughed.
I almost did, too.
But Mum always tells me
to be kind, so I tried.

I don't think it worked.
I said:

PURPLE is MY Favourite Colour.

I thought Tanisha would smile.
But she ran into the hall instead.

When she came back,
snack time was over.
She put on her art smock
and didn't look at anyone.

I almost told Tanisha that art was my favourite class,
but I didn't want her to leave again.
So I painted purple splotches and added some green
until I had a bunch of beautiful violets.

While I painted, I thought about Tanisha.

Should I have handed her my napkin?
Let her borrow my sweatshirt?
Spilled my juice so everyone stared at me instead?

What does it mean to be kind anyway?

Maybe it's giving.
Making cookies for Mr. Rinaldi, who lives alone.

Letting someone with smaller feet have my too-tight shoes.

(He might win races in them, too.)

Maybe it's helping.

Putting dirty dishes in the sink.

Cleaning up after Otis,
our class guinea pig.
(He's a messy eater.)

Maybe it's paying attention.

Telling Desmond I like his blue boots.

Asking the new girl to be my partner.

Listening to Aunt Franny's stories.
(Even the ones I've heard before.)

Being kind should be easy.
Like throwing away a wrapper
or recycling a bottle.

Or saying:

Being kind can be hard, too.
Even when you know what to do.
Teaching someone something I'm good at is tricky.

(Even when I'm patient.)

And sticking up
for someone when
other kids aren't kind
is really hard.

(And really scary.)

Maybe I can't solve Tanisha's grape juice problem.
Maybe all I can do is sit by her in art class.

And paint this picture for her.
Because I know she likes purple, too.

Maybe I can only do small things.

But my small things might join small things other people do.

And, together, they could grow into something big.

Something really big.
So big that all our kindnesses spill out of our school . . .

ANIMAL REFUGE

PUBLIC LIBRARY

BUS STOP

spread throughout town . . .

travel across the country...

and go all the way...

around the world.

Right back to Tanisha and me.
So we can be kind.

Again.

And again.

And again.